Puppy Love

Written by Rico Green

Illustrated by Tammie Lyon

Based on the character "Air Bud," created by Kevin DiCicco

Based on characters created by Robert Vince & Anna McRoberts

Disney PRESS

New York • Los Angeles

Printed in the United States of America

First Edition 1 3 5 7 9 10 8 6 4 2

ISBN 978-1-4231-7577-3

G658-7729-4-13305

Library of Congress Control Number: 2013946500

For more Disney Press fun, visit www.disneybooks.com

It was the day of the big Fernfield Valentine's Day Dance.
"I think it's a total bummer we don't have dates for the dance tonight,"
said Mudbud. "V-Day is all about chillin' with your one true love!"

Buddha shook his head. "It's okay to focus on your family and friends on Valentine's Day," he said. "Also, remember to love thyself."

"I'm not dancing with *myself* tonight," B-Dawg replied.

Just then, there was the loud creaking sound of a door being opened.

A poodle stepped out from the Leap Dog Dance Studio.
"'Bye, Tiffany, see you later!" another dog called to the poodle.

Tiffany trotted gracefully past the Buddies.
"Cute ballet shoes!" Rosebud said.
B-Dawg sighed. "She's a dancer, like me. I gotta meet her."

"Dude, she could be your one true love!" said Mudbud.

"Come on!" said Rosebud. "Go ask her to the dance!"

B-Dawg gazed after Tiffany.

"But *how* do I ask her to the dance?" he said.

"How about you give her a gift?" Mudbud suggested.

"Every dude and dudette likes a gift. Piece of cake!"

"That's it!" said Budderball. "Follow me!"
He led the Buddies to the bakery. Budderball
bought a big cake with hearts on it.
    "Give this to Tiffany. She'll love it!"

But then B-Dawg tripped over his own feet and fell face-first into the cake.
"Oh, brother," said Rosebud.
"This is nuts!" wailed B-Dawg. "Now what do I do?"

Next the Buddies went to a florist. "Hey," said Rosebud. "I know I love fresh flowers. Try giving Tiffany a glamorous bouquet!"

"I dig your thinkin'," said B-Dawg.

The Buddies helped gather some flowers for a bouquet.

When B-Dawg started walking with the flowers, a strong
winter wind gusted past him. It blew all the flower petals off!
He looked at the ruined flowers sadly.

"I do not believe that is what nature intended," said Buddha.

"Dude, don't give up," said Mudbud. "Write her a rap."

"Mudbud's right," said Rosebud. "You're a master rapper!"

B-Dawg smiled. "How about . . . *I like romance, I like ants. . . .*
Let's go to the dance—just take a chance?"

"Karma is not on your
side," said Buddha.

Then B-Dawg said, *"Roses are red, poison ivy is itchy;*
you make my whiskers . . . feel kind of twitchy!"

"My chi has been deeply
disturbed," said Buddha.

Soon it was almost time for the dance.

"I tried," said B-Dawg sadly. "Maybe it's not meant to be. Let's just forget about the whole thing."

VALENTINE'S DANCE

"We should all still go!" said Budderball. "There might be snacks there!"

"To dance is to channel one's good energy," said Buddha.

"Let's totally go," said Rosebud.

The Buddies walked toward the door.

"You guys go on in," said B-Dawg. "I'll be right there."

"We stick together, dude," said Mudbud. "Let's all go in."

"All right," said B-Dawg.

The Buddies went inside the gymnasium. Music played and couples spun on the dance floor. B-Dawg still couldn't believe that all his attempts to impress Tiffany had failed.

Suddenly, Tiffany appeared outside the door. She was still wearing the tutu she had worn earlier, and she was walking at top speed past the gymnasium.

B-Dawg realized she wasn't going to the dance at all!
"Go get her," said Rosebud. "We'll be right here!"

"Hey!" said B-Dawg. "Where are you going?"

He raced over to Tiffany. She looked back shyly but kept walking.

"Don't you love to dance?" B-Dawg asked. Tiffany turned and looked at B-Dawg.

"That's just it," Tiffany said. "I don't know how to dance. That's why I've been taking lessons at the Leap Dog Dance Studio. Oh, I'm so embarrassed!" She whimpered and started to run away.

"Wait! Come back!" called B-Dawg. "I can *teach* you!"

Tiffany tried to move around B-Dawg.

Left. Right. Left.

He kept matching her moves. She jumped this way and that.
"Hey," B-Dawg said with a smile. "You're dancing!"

Tiffany froze. "I am?"

"Totally," he said.

She moved left, then right. "Hey . . . this is easy!"

"You're a natural!" he said. "Want to join me inside?"

"Sure!" Tiffany said as she followed B-Dawg into the gymnasium.

The Buddies met Tiffany, and they all danced and had a great time at the Valentine's Day Dance.